For Enrique

www.mascotbooks.com

The Lying, Lying Lion

©2015 Kerry Morris. All Rights Reserved. No part of this publication may
be reproduced, stored in a retrieval system or transmitted in any form
by any means electronic, mechanical, or photocopying, recording or
otherwise without the permission of the author.

For more information, please contact:
Mascot Books
560 Herndon Parkway #120
Herndon, VA 20170
info@mascotbooks.com

Library of Congress Control Number: 2015913847

CPSIA Code: PRT1015A
ISBN-13: 978-1-63177-323-5

Printed in the United States

The Lying, Lying Lion

by **Kerry Morris**
Illustrated by Taylor Freshley

The head lion roared. It was heard over five miles in every direction. As the only cats that live in groups, the lions awaited the others to arrive for an emergency Big Cat Council.

The cheetahs, the world's fastest land mammals, arrived first. One went from zero to sixty miles per hour in three seconds and landed beside them faster than the lions could say "cheetah".

The leopards came slinking out of the trees at the savannah's edge. They were the strongest climbers, sleeping, hunting, and even eating in trees after dragging their food up. They rasped to announce their presence.

The servals, the cats of spare parts, ambled in on their long legs. As they waited, one at the back leapt ten feet in the air and clapped its paws around a flying bird.

The caracals emerged from the grass, camouflaged by the tufts of hair on their ears until they were quite close.

"We are all here," proclaimed the lion. "I called this council to discuss the territorial treaty. We are losing more habitat, and we must work together to survive."

Something rustled in the grass and all the cats hissed.

Hoss stumbled out and froze. The cats were puzzled. With his lion cut, Hoss resembled one of them, but they knew something wasn't quite right. "Who are you?!" boomed the head lion.

"My name is Hoss. I'm a Tibetan Mastiff, and I'm on a safari. Excuse my haircut. It is just so hot!"

A young, scrawny lion padded up. "He...sneaked past me. Er, he threatened and tried to hurt me!"

"Silence, you lazy, lying lion! You weren't keeping watch!" The other cats growled. "This is the last time. You are banished!"

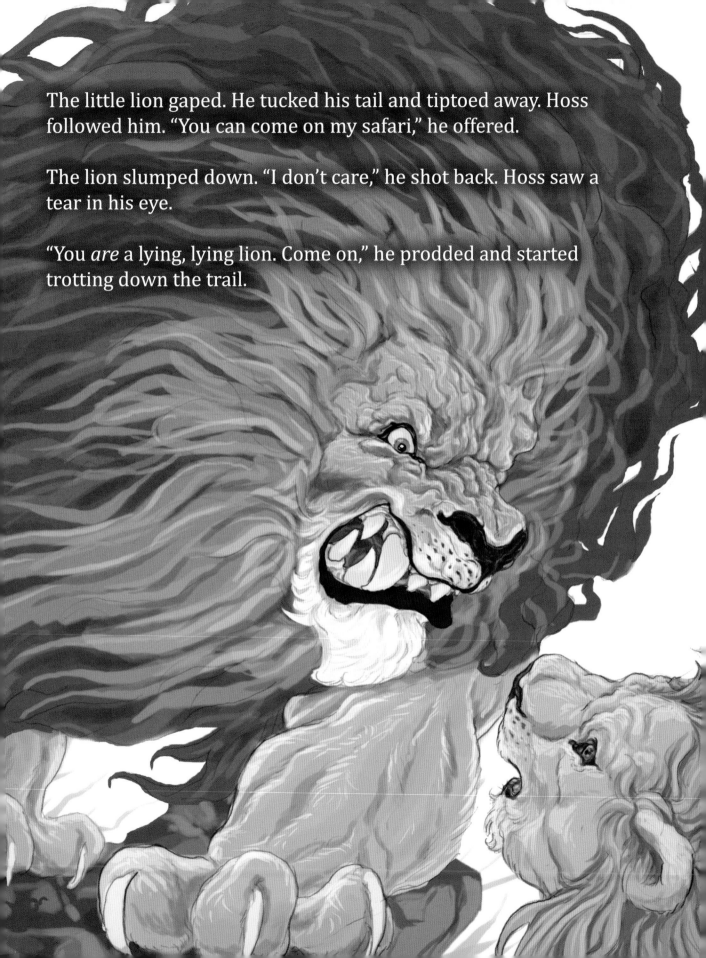

The little lion gaped. He tucked his tail and tiptoed away. Hoss followed him. "You can come on my safari," he offered.

The lion slumped down. "I don't care," he shot back. Hoss saw a tear in his eye.

"You *are* a lying, lying lion. Come on," he prodded and started trotting down the trail.

in the midday heat, Hoss and the lion took a break in the shade. "Is this the famous umbrella tree?" Hoss asked.

"You mean the acacia? No, it's a desert fig. They look similar, but you can tell the difference by the green thorns and fruit."

Hoss reared up to taste a low-hanging fig, but at the last moment a greedy hand swiped it.

A band of banded mongoose bandits descended upon them. There were at least forty scurrying in every direction, snatching up the figs, seizing all the bugs and debris in sight, stealing Hoss' safari supplies, stuffing their hands and mouths full as possible. They scuttled away, huffing and howling victoriously.

"You didn't even help! You just laid there!" Hoss chided as the lazy lion yawned. "You must learn that it takes hard work to earn and protect. And anything worth earning and protecting is worth the hard work."

They roamed over rolling plains. "Serengeti means 'endless plains' in the Maasai language. That's certainly how it feels," complained the lion.

In a grassy field, they found a pack of hyenas playing soccer. It was spots versus stripes, and the hyenas were wailing at each other to pass the ball. It was accidentally kicked to Hoss. When it stopped rolling, the ball unfurled into an animal with golden scales. Hoss jumped. The hyenas laughed. "Don't laugh at us!" shouted the lion.

A tall, spotted female trotted over. "We're not laughing at you. Our laughter is an alert that there is food nearby. We like to play hard, but there are times to work hard too." The hyenas darted off to hunt and scavenge.

The soccer ball still stood there. "Don't mind her. Females are the leaders amongst hyenas. She is this clan's matriarch." He waddled to an anthill and jammed a long, sticky tongue that had been curled in a chest pouch into the cracks. "Hold on," he muttered as he collected and swallowed some sand and stones. "I'm a ground pangolin. I don't have teeth so the sand grinds up my food."

"Didn't that sting?" asked the lion.

"I have my scales, tough eyelids, closable nostrils, and internal ears so they can't bite me." He yawned, his sticky tongue flicking out again. "Time for bed! I am nocturnal, so I sleep in my burrow during the day. I only came out for the soccer game. Like the lady said: work hard and play hard! Goodnight!"

Hoss and the lion reached a river with trembling banks. On the other side, thousands of wildebeests were running along the edge, selecting a place to cross. "The Great Migration!" Hoss exclaimed.

"It is called the greatest show on Earth," the lion responded. "1.5 million wildebeests and half a million zebras, gazelles, elands, and impalas migrate every year."

"Wildebeests!" the lion growled as he hunched his shoulders. "They're so hard to catch. Even the newborns walk within a couple of minutes and can run after only five. They outrun some of our best lionesses soon after."

"Too much hard work, lazy lion?" teased Hoss.

The lion glared, then dared, "I could catch one. I'm done being lazy and unhelpful." He took off with a playful shove, and the two chased wildebeests the rest of the evening, laughing like hyenas, playing and working hard at the same time.

Thirsty, Hoss and the lion were happy to reach Lake Victoria. It was the largest African lake and the largest tropical lake in the world. They lapped at the water beside a jackal. Suddenly, the water surged as an enormous, scaly crocodile exploded out. "You've got me!" cried the jackal. "I'll challenge you to a game of wit and rhyming for my freedom. Will you gamble?"

The crocodile smiled, his sharp teeth glistening. "You first!"

"I'm Jack, the black-backed jackal
I have a knack so have no lack
Rhyme upon rhyme I tack and stack
Till you're taken aback, thrown off track
You don't want me for a snack
I'd make you smack, your jaws crack,
Your teeth would get plaque
Plus my pack is back in that bivouac
They'll know of your attack
And give you flack with no slack
I have more rhymes in my sack
I could unpack, if you think you can hack."

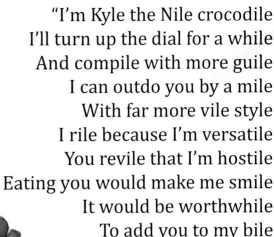

"I'm Kyle the Nile crocodile
I'll turn up the dial for a while
And compile with more guile
I can outdo you by a mile
With far more vile style
I rile because I'm versatile
You revile that I'm hostile
Eating you would make me smile
It would be worthwhile
To add you to my bile
Yet another file in my pile
I think it's time for our trial."

"Who won?" Hoss asked.

The lion squinted in concentration. The crocodile rattled his teeth.
The jackal trembled. "The jackal. He had one more rhyme."

"You're right," admitted the crocodile. "Your honesty saved him.
Sometimes truth is a matter of life and death."

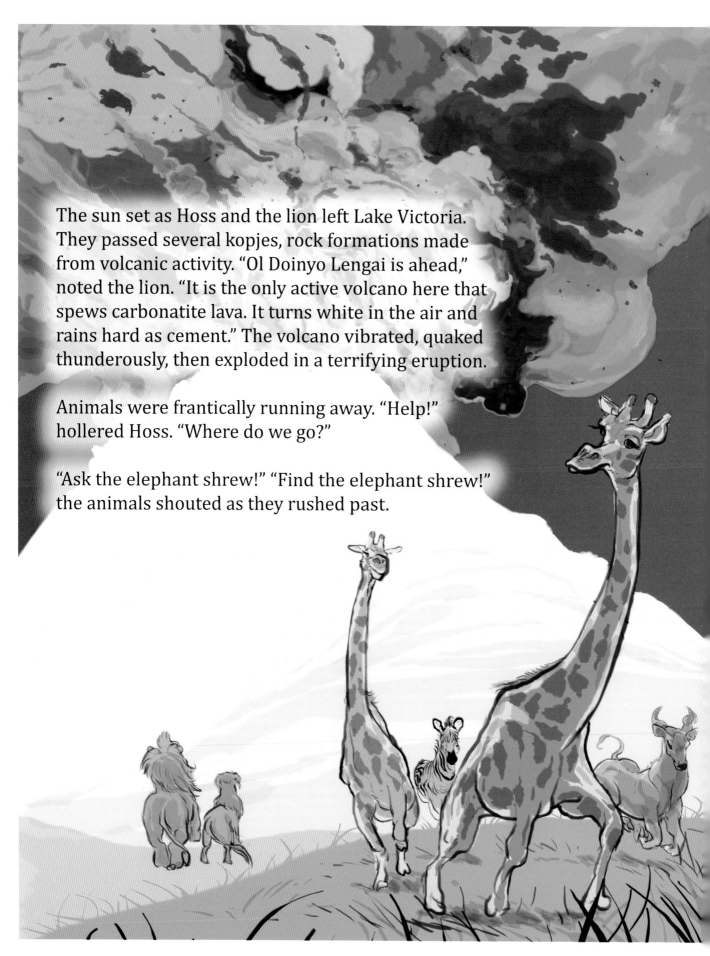

The sun set as Hoss and the lion left Lake Victoria. They passed several kopjes, rock formations made from volcanic activity. "Ol Doinyo Lengai is ahead," noted the lion. "It is the only active volcano here that spews carbonatite lava. It turns white in the air and rains hard as cement." The volcano vibrated, quaked thunderously, then exploded in a terrifying eruption.

Animals were frantically running away. "Help!" hollered Hoss. "Where do we go?"

"Ask the elephant shrew!" "Find the elephant shrew!" the animals shouted as they rushed past.

They saw an elephant lumbering in the distance. As the largest land mammal, she stood out from the others. They caught up and slowed to a trot. "Excuse me, Ms. Shrew the elephant—?"

"What? You're mistaken. My name isn't Shrew."

"Please!" shouted Hoss. "We are looking for the elephant, Shrew!"

"Here I am," a tiny voice squeaked behind them. The elephant shrew did have a long, trunk-like nose but otherwise they looked nothing alike.

"We were told you could lead us to safety," urged the lion.

"I can! I have several paths cleared through my territory for hunting insects. Follow me. But keep up! I run and jump like an antelope on my speedways and you must follow the true path to escape."

They ran and ran, working the hardest yet. In the end, they narrowly escaped.

Exhausted, Hoss and the lion collapsed in some brush and slept through the night. Hoss awoke to stomping sounds. Feather quills, like old secretary pens, bobbed over the bushes. Hoss nudged the lion awake and they crept out to investigate.

A secretary bird was running to and fro on its long, gangly legs. "Hello?" Hoss called.

"Hello! No time to talk. I'm running errands for the black rhinoceros. Time is of the essence!" He ran off in a straight line, picking up speed as on a runway before he took flight and drifted over the horizon.

They heard grunting nearby. Through some leaves, sitting in a mud pool, was the black rhino.

"He's gray and he looks like a dinosaur," noted the lion.

"A dinosaur?" the rhino chuckled. "We are the oldest land mammals, so we look prehistoric. Come out," he commanded. "I am gray. Strangely, so is the white rhino. Our difference is our lip shapes and that they are larger. I mean...*he* is larger." The great rhino grew sad. "There is only one male Northern white rhino left. His name is Sudan. We are on a mission to save him and his kind from greedy poaching for our horns."

Hoss and the lion gasped. The black rhino had one horn left and a scar farther up his snout.

The black rhino moaned. "Sometimes the truth is very hard to face. It is easier to ignore or retell it in a happier way. But we must be brave and face the truth so we can act from it."

A couple of tears flowed from the lion's wide eyes. They listened to the wise, strong black rhino's stories for a long time. As they left, they softly nosed the rhino's remaining horn with respect and compassion.

With full hearts, Hoss and the lion made their way back. Hoss' safari was over, and the lion was ready to prove himself as hardworking and honest. The Big Cat Council was back in session. The felines frowned as the lying, lying lion stepped into the circle. "You are not welcome here!" a serval catcalled.

"I have come to apologize and ask for a second chance. I am ready to take responsibility for my actions and for myself. Please let me prove my place in the pride." The lion bowed nobly.

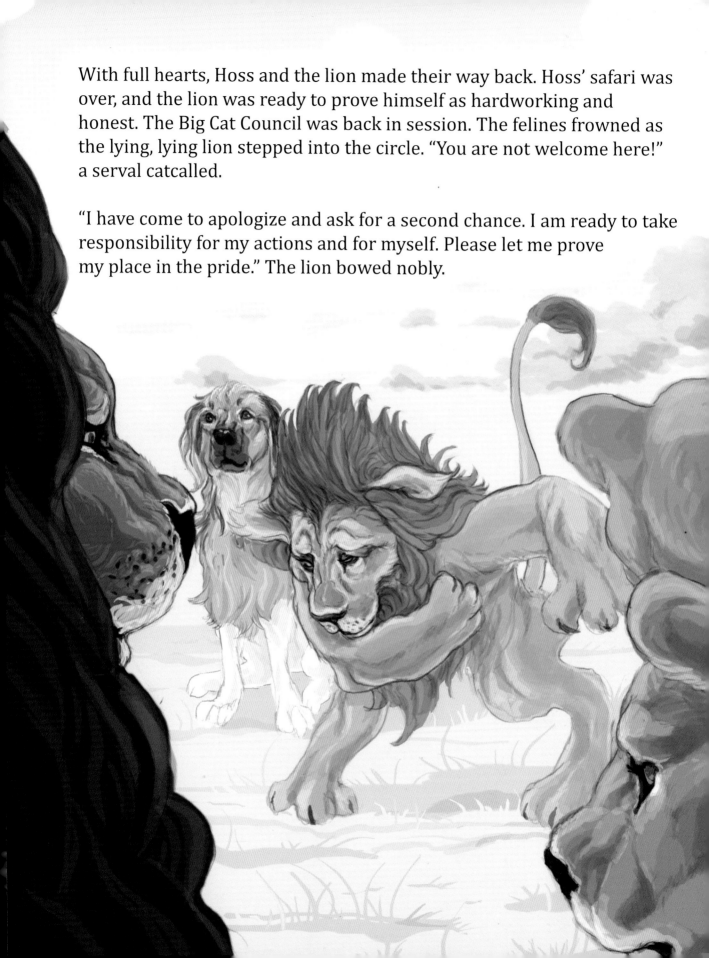

The big cats welcomed him back warmly. They gave him a new job to demonstrate his new character, patrolling the territorial lines.

"I will be like you, patrolling and protecting with honor," the lion blushed when he told Hoss. He walked Hoss to the end of the Serengeti to say goodbye. As he turned to go, the lion shouted, "Work hard!"

"Play hard!" Hoss winked back.

"Act from truth!"

About the Author

Kerry works, studies, writes, and walks Hoss in Texas. Believe it or not, it gets hotter than the Serengeti in the summer, so he gets a lion cut to stay cool!